THE
DREADED ONES

The Dreaded Ones is a work of fiction. References to real people, events, establishments, organizations, or locales are intended only to provide the sense of authenticity and are use fictitiously. All other characters, all incidents, dialogue are drawn from the author's imagination and are not to be seen as real.

Copyright © 2022 by Ty'Ron W. C. Robinson II. All rights reserved.

Published by Dark Titan Publishing. A division of Dark Titan Entertainment.

Also available in eBook.

Dark Titan Extended is a branch of Dark Titan Entertainment.

Paperback ISBN: 979-8-9856344-4-0
eBook ISBN: 979-8-9856344-5-7

darktitanentertainment.com

WORKS BY TY'RON W. C. ROBINSON II

BOOKS/SHORT STORIES

DARK TITAN UNIVERSE SAGA

MAIN SERIES
Dark Titan Knights
The Resistance Protocol
Tales of the Scattered
Tales of the Numinous
Day of Octagon
Crossbreed
Heaven's Called
The Oranos Imperative
Underworld

SPIN-OFFS
In A Glass of Dawn: The Casebook of Travis Vail
Maveth: Bloodsport
The Curse of The Mutant-Thing
Trail of Vengeance
War of The Thunder Gods

ONE-SHOTS
Maveth, The Death-Bringer Mystery of The Mutant-Thing Shade & Switchblade
Retribution of Cain
The Mythologists
Ambush Bot
Kang-Zhu
Cheeseburger Man
Tessa Balthazar
Elite 5

COLLECTIONS
Dark Titan Omnibus: Volume 1 Dark Titan Omnibus: Volume 2
Dark Titan Universe Saga Spinoffs Omnibus: Volume 1
Dark Titan One-Shot Collection Dark Titan One-Shot Collection II

THE HAUNTED CITY SAGA
The Legendary Warslinger: The Haunted City I
Battle of Astolat: A Haunted City Prequel
Redemption of the Lost: The Haunted City II
Helper's Hand: A Haunted City One-Shot

SYMBOLUM VENATORES
Symbolum Venatores: The Gabriel Kane Collection
Hod: A Symbolum Venatores Book
Symbolum Venatores: War of The Two Kingdoms
Symbolum Venatores: Elrad's Chronicles

EVERWAR UNIVERSE
EverWar Universe: Knights & Lords

PRODIGIOUS WORLDS
Mark Porter of Argoron
Raiders of Vanok
Praxus of Lithonia

FRIGHTENED! SERIES
Frightened!: The Beginning

INSTINCTS SERIES
Lost in Shadows: Remastered

THE HORDE TRILOGY
The Horde

DARK TITAN'S THE DEAD DAYS
Accounts of The Dead Days

OTHER BOOKS
The Book of The Elect
The Extended Age Omnibus
The Eleventh Hour: A Chevah Mythos Story
The Supreme Pursuer: Darkness of the Hunt
Massacre in the Dusk
Venture into Horror: Tales of the Supernatural
The Universe of Realms Omnibus: Book 1
The Universe of Realms Omnibus: Book 2
Dark Titan Universe Coloring Book
Dark Titan: Universe of Realms Puzzle Book

THE DARK TITAN AUDIO EXPERIENCE PODCAST
Season 1: Introductions
Season 2: In a Glass of Dawn
Season 2.5: Accounts of The Dead Days
Season 3: Battle For Astolat
Season 4: Hallow Sword: Cursed

THE
DREADED ONES

TY'RON W. C. ROBINSON II

CONTENTS

CHAPTER ONE 1
CHAPTER TWO 3
CHAPTER THREE...5
CHAPTER FOUR..7
CHAPTER FIVE 12
CHAPTER SIX 16
CHAPTER SEVEN...19
CHAPTER EIGHT...25

BONUS: CREED: HELL RISEN 30

CHAPTER ONE

Two months. Two months have passed since the eclipse over Seattle, Washington. The vampires scurried themselves through the city, slaughtering many who were in their path. The streets were sealed off and the air travel was frozen. There was no way in or out of Seattle. However, Dr. Allan Desportan, Abelard Ekkehardt, and Lucy Seward remained alongside Anna Ilario and Brant Wade as they confronted Dunkan The Dark One. Running from the vampires and taking them out, the group found themselves near the outskirts of the city. Making their escape, they found a way out of the city and retreated into the wilderness. Moving south as they arrived in Olympia, Washington.

"What have you learned so far?" Dr. Allan Desportan asked Brant Wade.

"The military isn't aware of what's happening. I'm not sure why."

Throughout the weeks which had followed, the group had several run-ins with scattered vampires. While they did eliminate them, Lucy desired to study their anatomy as they dragged several vampire bodies into a shack. Lucy went and studied their vampiric changes to the human body as she began to learn more concerning their feeding patterns as well as their enhanced reflexes and agility.

"It rewrites the entire body." Lucy told Allan.
"Basically, reforming them as if they're being reborn?"
"To a degree."

Through their patience and longsuffering of the events unfolding, news had spread of the electricity returning to Seattle and once the National Guard had arrived, They found the city deserted. The downtown streets empty. Neither were there human or animal moving throughout. A sign of concern as they discovered trails of blood within the city limits all heading out onto the interstate, moving south.

Throughout the weeks which had followed, Desportan entered Olympia and saw nothing which would alarm him of a vampire appearance. Until, one day when he went into a coffee shop and sat down. Gazing up toward the TV, the Olympia news broadcast revealed a body was found near the entrance into the city and the victim's body was drained of blood. Quickly, Desportan stood up and left the shop. It was only a matter of time. Not weeks or months. Days.

CHAPTER TWO

After making his way back to the others, Desportan began to tell them of what he had seen. Hearing his words and the horror beneath them, they knew the vampires would only be near them sooner than anticipated. Abelard immediately stood up from his chair and looked out the window toward the woods. Giving the others a glare, they knew what he was about to say. Yet, Desportan stopped him before he could speak a word.

"We can't keep doing this."

"Doing what?" Lucy questioned.

"Keep moving place to place. This isn't right. We can stop this wherever we are."

"Seems you still do not understand the dangers we're all facing. We must move to avoid them. At any cost."

"We tried that already, remember. We left Seattle and look now, they've reached Olympia within a matter of weeks. Not months. Weeks!"

"Look, Allan." Lucy paused. "It was only a matter of time. We know they were going to migrate. It's not that different than birds during the changing seasons."

"These are not birds, Lucy. They're vampires. Literal vampires."

Abelard sighed.

"Where's your strength, Dr. Desportan?"

"My strength?"

"Yes. Because before we left Seattle, you were ready for the fight against the vampires. Now, after hearing the news of them within our reach, you decide to make a run for it."

"Because we are not fully equipped to handle a horde of vampires. A dozen of them maybe. But not hundreds or even thousands."

"Then that settles things." Abelard said.

"What do you mean, Professor?" Brant asked. "We take them all on. Face them till the death?"

"You would like that wouldn't you." Desportan chuckled. "We're not scarifying ourselves to them on some whim of a victory. We need a plan. A serious, operational plan."

"My plan is simple. We head south. Into Oregon. There's a place there I've frequent before during my travels in this region of the country. Salem. We head there and recruit new soldiers for this fight."

"So, you're going to go into this town and ask people if they're willing to join us in fighting them?"

"Yes."

"And how are you certain they'll believe you?"

"Because, they're aware of the vampires' existence. I helped them out several years ago in ridding a nest in their territory. Although, the vampires I encountered there were unlike the ones we've recently dealt with."

"Wait. Hold on. Unlike the others? You're saying there's a different breed of vampires aside from the horde we encountered led by this Dark One?"

"Yes. I'll explain more once we get there. Perhaps, the people will as well."

CHAPTER THREE

While the group had packed their belongings and left for Salem, Oregon. Scurrying through the wilderness were a pack of vampires. Only these showed more of a pale feature. They had no hair, appearing to look like albinos, yet their skin was shedding and portions of their bones were visible. If one were to encounter these vampires, one would accuse them of being zombies, especially in their rushing speed. A dozen of them ran through the trees and toward a cave as thunder cracked above them. The pale ones rushed toward a pillar in the cave. The pillar appeared to be a natural one made with the cave itself. The pale ones paused and bowed their heads as a looming figure began to move toward them from the other side of the pillar. Walking slowly, the figure shared the same features as the pale ones. Decayed flesh, sharp fangs, and pale skin. Although, this one wore garments which resembled the Colonial period.

"The time is upon us!" The figure spoke. "The Dark One's essence has filled the air. His workings in the larger city have shown us we can win this war. I speak on this day, I, Aldrik, leader of you all shall march with you into battle against these so-called Fated Ones. For the battle has begun and the war will be ours!"

The pale ones snare in a victorious screech. Howling like wolves with the sound of the thunder. Aldrik, their leader grinned with his sharp fangs showing. His eyes appeared dead, yet within the retinas were a glimmer of life. Life not of human nature, but something much darker.

CHAPTER FOUR

The group make their arrival in Salem, Oregon and within only a matter of minutes, a collage of people ran through the streets in terror. Desportan exited the vehicle, trying to ask the scattering people about their concerns. Neither answered him a word, for they only screamed as he reached out to them. Others bumping him to get away from whatever horrified them.

"Dr. Desportan." Abelard said. "Get back in the car now."

Desportan refused to heed Abelard's concerning words as he continued to stop the civilians, begging for an answer. Looking ahead into the streets, one civilian pointed and ran. What Desportan had seen were seven vampires. Their clothing was torn, however their skin was not pale nor decaying. Desportan knew these vampires had come from Seattle.

"They've made it even here." Desportan said.

Brant and Anna exited the vehicle and began taking fire toward the vampires. Abelard stepped out of the car and joined them in taking out the vampires. Lucy even stepped out of the car and stood beside Desportan, handing him a handgun. Seeing the others firing, Desportan joined in with the lowering screams of the people lingering behind him.

Moving with a slight tingling of fear, his determination was clear as he ran into the fight, firing shots toward the snarling vampires. With the team all fighting against the vampires, a stranger rushed into the firefight on the right side of Desportan with a shotgun, blasting the heads of the vampires into pieces. Desportan stopped his shooting as the stranger eliminated the vampires on his own. A moment of silence filled the air as the stranger turned back and approached them.

"Nice going with the shotgun." Desportan said. "Aldon."

With a smirk on his face, Aldon turned toward Desportan and nodded gently.

"Figured I would do some good around here. Ever since these things showed up, I've been preparing for this moment."

Lucy saw Aldon and approached him beside Desportan, hugging him with a smile on her face. Behind them was Abelard making his approach.

"Good to see you again." Lucy said.

"Same I say of you."

"You've been preparing?" Abelard asked as he approached. "You knew of the vampires?"

"I heard what happened in Seattle. Figured it wouldn't be long before they make their way south. And as you can see, they have."

"And you've pretty much helped these people before the vampires' arrival?" Desportan said.

"Not quite. The people didn't believe me when I told them about the goings of Seattle. They brushed it off as some kind of story idea I made up. I was a writer in the years prior. Wrote about horror and suchlike."

"Seeing these vamps makes it look like your stories have come to life." Brant joked.

"In a way, it appears to be the case." Aldon glanced at his watch.

"Need to be somewhere in a hurry?" Desportan asked.

"Yeah. My homestead. I need to make sure everything is in place."

"Your homestead?" Anna said.

"I see you've achieved it." Desportan smiled. "Good job."

"You have a set of land to yourself?" Abelard questioned.

"Yes. Purchased it off my book sales. It was one of my goals."

"He always spoke about having a homestead of his own." Desportan spoke. "Is it far from civilization in a way like you wanted? Like far enough for the vampires to not have reached?"

"It is."

"So, I take it's guarded up. Protected around every barrier possible?" Abelard said. "Almost like a fortress."

"I've done my best. Hopefully, it can keep the place secured."

"Hey Doc," Brant said. "Why don't we tag along with this guy. He has a homestead. I mean, we do need some place to gather ourselves before we make our next plan."

"You just arrived into Salem?"

"Yes we did. Out of the possibility of encountering more vampires. Yet, you've already seen we didn't' achieve what we wished for."

Aldon nodded.

"Alright then. Get in your car and follow me."

The team entered the vehicle as Desportan continued to talk with Aldon. The stranger had informed him of others at the homestead and it gave Desportan some comfort. Before returning to the car.

Following Aldon through the roads of Salem and back out into the wilderness of Oregon, the team had made their arrival at Aldon's homestead. A large ranch with a two-story home. Exiting the vehicle, the team looked at the ranch and the home. Brant was amazed. He never been on a ranch nor that far out from the city.

"The surroundings are well guarded. Far out from the public eye. Open fields for one to keep eyes on." Abelard said. "Good work."

"This is a nice place." Lucy said.

"Thank you, Lucy. It provides me well with the silence. Peace is something I often seek."

"That makes two of us." Desportan replied. "You did well for yourself."

"Now, if you'll follow me, I'll show you the inside."

Walking into the home, the group see one man sitting on the couch, reading one of Aldon's books. The man raised his eyes toward the door as they entered. He looked at Aldon before his eyes wandered toward the others.

"Hey, Aldon, how come this book of yours doesn't have a sequel yet?"

"Because it's not yet written."

"Ah. And who are they?" Abelard wondered.

"Allies in this fight against the vampires."

"Oh." The man stood up and approached the team, extending his hand. "My name's Eddie. Eddie Rain."

"Dr. Allan Desportan."

"Desportan? What kind of name is that?"

"A rare one."

"And you are?" Eddie asked Abelard."

"Professor Abelard Ekkehardt, hunter of the vampires."

"Ekkehardt? Hey, Aldon, what's with your guests' names?"

"Ekkehardt has a long history across Europe." Abelard grinned. "It'll stick after a while."

"No need to instruct him, Professor." Brant said. "He'll be fine."

"I'll instruct you to your rooms and we can talk after."

"Good with me." Desportan said.

"With me as well." Abelard said. "We have a lot to discuss."

Walking up the stairs, Aldon presents five rooms. Desportan and Lucy took a room to share, Anna grabbed a room, Abelard took the room next to Anna's. Brant grabbed the room next to

Desportan and Lucy's. The fifth room was all that remained.

"And who might have that one?" Desportan asked.

"Any others that might come across us. To join us in this fight."

"Judging by your tone, you've taken this seriously." Abelard said.

"I have. I've only written about vampires in my stories. But, what I've seen these past two months has shown me much in this world exists that society has not yet been willing to accept."

"Well, it seems you're on the same boat with us once again." Desportan said. "I too did not believe in all this vampire shit before I had my first contact."

"I told you when I met you," Abelard said. "These things are real and to accept the reality they bring with them."

"I guess we can all talk after dinner. Donn went out to prepare the food."

"Donn?"

"Another one of us who's joined in the fight. He's a hunter. Archery and all."

"Archery will prove a useful skill against the vampires." Abelard nodded. "Good choice of skill."

"When we eat, we can discuss everything we need to know concerning the vampires."

Elsewhere far from the homestead, Aldrik stood in a field with his vampire horde around him. Their snarls had driven the animals from the woods around them as did their stench. The smell of decay. The odor of death. Aldrik took a breath and sighed.

"I can sense you, Dark One. I know where you are."

CHAPTER FIVE

Upon waiting, Donn entered the home as he saw the group sitting with Aldon in the living room. Standing up to greet him, Aldon informed Donn of the visitors and their aid to the cause of the vampires. Donn, hearing the words became astonished. Seeing others getting into the fight for the better was something he desired ever since the vampires first appeared.

Sitting down to eat dinner, the group talked amongst themselves, questioning Aldon on his choices concerning the vampires and his plans for the days ahead. Sitting at the table with them were both Donn and Eddie. Aldon had told Desportan and Abelard of the two others' previous home: Seattle.

"You were both from Seattle?" Desportan asked.

"Yeah. Although, we didn't encounter each other until we met up with Aldon. Became a three-person unit of hunters. Took out some vampires in Seattle before making our escape to this place."

"You've slaughtered some on your travels?" Abelard asked Donn.

"I did. My bow helped me get them from afar."

"Ah. Good choice. Knew it."

"Now, what is your plan for stopping these vampires from overtaking your homestead?" Desportan asked.

Aldon nodded with a calm expression. Taking a breath.

"Simple. The three of us here will hold them off."

"But what if you're unable to match their speed? Their tenacity? Their sheer lack of humanity?" Abelard said. "As you have noticed during your times out there, these vampires move in such a speed incapable by our own admonition."

"I think with the skills we possess, we'll do ourselves well in the fight." Eddie replied. "Besides, what have you guys done since arriving in Salem?"

"For starters," Desported answered. "we were present to the vampires after encountering them in a tunnel back in Seattle after the interstate incident."

"Ah." Donn said. "The interstate. Isn't that where all of this began in the first place?"

"It goes back much further in time, my friend." Abelard said. "Such a time you would not even believe."

"How far back?" Eddie wondered. "Like several months ago or a year?"

"He's speaking of centuries." Brant pointed. "Dude's been hunting down these vampires since he was a young one."

Abelard nodded with a smirk. What Brant had said was true.

"The vampires have a long history in this world. Far beyond the history you've been taught in schools."

"So, these vampires have been around since ancient times." Donn said. "I'm intrigued. Perhaps, they were involved in some of history's greatest events."

"More than involved in some I can concur."

Aldon took a liking to Abelard. His knowledge of the vampires intrigued him to know more. From there, Aldon sat at the table and began asking several questions regarding the vampires' origin in the States to Abelard's encounters with them over in Eastern Europe. Abelard was not afraid to hide what he knew. He always wanted to share his knowledge to those with serious intent on eliminating the vampires from the world. Once dinner was complete, everyone sat in the living room area as Abelard began telling stories of his adventures as well as some history of the vampires.

"Where to begin." Abelard chuckled. "Ah. I know. When I was a young lad, in my mid-twenties, me and a friend had come to discover a cave during the late portions of Winter. Caves during those days were forbidden to the public, unless you worked in the mines. Only once we arrived, there was no mining equipment laying around. Nothing but rocks, dirt, and snow."

"Did you guys go inside?" Donn wondered.

"We did. When we first entered the cave, the darkness overtook us. To the point where we fled from the cave and went to grab lamps to give us sight. I knew then from the darkness there was something otherworld inside the cave. Only I didn't have the knowledge to know what I had to do. We went back into the cave. This time we walked deeper, the lamps' light helped us make moves. As we searched the cave, we caught the scent of blood in the air. Mixed with the rocks and dirt. At that moment, my friend grabbed me and pointed ahead. What we saw had terrified the both of us."

"What did you see?" Lucy asked.

"We saw our first vampire. Cloaked in its own shadow. Feasting on a missing woman's corpse. Ripping the flesh from her bones as it continued to gnawed on her throat.

"Did you guys kill it?" Eddie wondered.

Abelard chuckled under his breath. His eyes blinking repeatedly as he took the second to speak forth his response. A sigh exhaled from his being as he nodded toward Eddie.

"We did. Eventually."

"Eventually?" Brant said. "You guys ran or something?"

"You tell me what would you do in your first encounter with a vampire. Especially one as powerful as the Dark One."

"The Dark One." Desportan said. "He's the one you and your friend saw in the cave?"

"Yes. That snowy day was my first encounter with the Dark One. His power could even be felt outside the cave walls."

"I felt the same energy the night we left Seattle." Desportan said. 'A dark, cold presence. It felt as if he could see us wherever we were. Like he was walking beside us."

"That is due to his vampire horde he has created."

"This Dark One you speak of," Aldon said. "he's out there creating vampires for what? To take over the world?"

"Precisely." Abelard replied. "It is his sole purpose to fill the earth with his kind."

"It all makes sense." Donn said. "We kill this Dark One, we kill his vampire spawn."

Abelard paused Donn's talk as he raised his hand.

"Such an action is not simple."

Desportan gazed out toward the window, seeing the moon ahead. Aldon took a glance as well for his own measure and the two nodded.

"Best we get some sleep." Desportan said. "Plan out our next steps in the morning."

"I agree." Aldon said. "Sleep for the night. Prep in the morning."

Everyone had went to their place of dwelling and slept for the night. While Desportan's crew had slept, Donn remained awake as he watched the perimeter of the homestead. His eyes moving through the darkness around them. His eyes were set and his weapons were ready.

CHAPTER SIX

Through the night hours only silence covered the grounds of Aldon's homestead. Donn continued his watch as from the corner of his eye something slithered through the trees nearby . Donn paused in his place and held up his bow, slowly reaching for an arrow as the moving through the trees had continued. This time he saw them straight ahead. Moe movement increased as shadow figures barricaded the home. The sound of glass shattering awoke the others as they heard Donn's scream for assistance followed by snarls and fired arrows.

"Tine for you all to wake up! We have company!"

They rushed outside of the room, hearing Donn shooting arrows with thuds sounding afterwards. Running downstairs, they see Donn killing several vampires. Abelard's eyes widen, moving the others away as he raised his blade to kill with Anna doing the same.

"Vampires." Desportan said.

"How did they find us?" Brant wondered.

"That's not the topic for discussion." Aldon said. "We have to get them out of here."

"We must slaughter them!" Abelard yelled. "Everyone pick a target!"

"You don't have to ask me twice." Brant said, cocking the shotgun.

"We have no choice." Desportan said to Aldon.

The two agreed and aided in the fight. As more vampires were killed, others came from the shattered windows. Their fangs shown and their eyes glowing red. Brant moved through the vampires near the front door, blasting them with a shotgun.

"Come on! Keep on coming you bastards!"

Donn made his move to the top of the stairs and fired arrows through the heads of the vampires entering from the windows. Anna stood next to Abelard as they took out the vampires with their blades. Desportan, Eddie, and Aldon used their guns to blow off the heads of the vampires. Through their appearing victory, more vampires emerged from the tree line. It was almost as if the more vampires were killed, the double of them would appear.

"There's too many of them." Aldon said.

"We have no choice but to survive." Abelard replied. "We kill them all!"

The vampire horde outside of the home inched closer toward the windows. One of the vampires reached the window as its arm latched onto the broken glass on the side. Sticking its head through the opening and snarling toward the group before it was quickly pulled away. The silence in the home caused everyone to question what was happening as the vampires' gaze turned to something else outside of the home. Their snarls and screeches emitted the sound of fear as they were taken out by something else moving through the darkness. The sound of a rushing wind echoed from the outside, burying the vampire screeches into silence.

"What's happening?" Eddie asked.

"They're gone?" Lucy wondered. "There's nothing outside. No sound.

"I'm not too sure." Desportan said. "Dr. Ekkehardt? Any ideas?"

"No. None that I would consider possible."

"It's like something spooked them." Brant said. "Any idea what could've done that?"

"There's a plethora of things that could've scared them off." Abelard said. "I'm not certain on what could've done that during the night."

"Well, whatever it was, it quickly grabbed the attention. Took them off of us." Desportan said. "I say that is something good."

Donn walked down the stairs. The bow steady in his hand tightly as he grabbed another arrow.

"I'll go have a look." Donn said walking toward the front door.

"I'm coming with." Brant said, following him.

Unaware of what took place, outside the home laid the bodies of the vampires. Their heads decapitated. The rushing sound had moved into the sky and above the home hovered Aldrik and his vampire army. His army was keen to bolt down into the home, yet Aldrik stopped them.

CHAPTER SEVEN

Stepping to the outside, Brant and Donn caught the sight of the dead vampires. Their bodies covered in blood as their heads were scattered across the field. Donn approached the bodies and checked them. Brant did the same as he held the shotgun, aimed to the opposite direction. Brant was cautious, yet prepared. Donn was the same, only calmer.

"The hell did all of this?" Brant questioned. "Decapitated every single one of them."

"Something powerful." Donn said. "Something just as powerful as themselves."

"Any bears in this area?"

"I'm not sure one bear could've taken them all out at once."

"Of course." Brant scoffed. "But something came through here. Something big."

Donn kicked one of the heads as he rose up from the ground, brushing himself off. Taking a glance into the sky, he saw the moon and something moved past it. A shadow of sorts. Brushing it off, Donn and Brant returned to the home.

"Find anything?" Aldon asked.

"Dead vampires." Donn said. "All of them."

"All of them?" Abelard said. "Are you certain?"

"Yeah. Every last one of them." Brant said. "Had their heads chopped off."

Abelard nodded as he went and sat down at the dinner table. Sighing.

"I do not understand. What could've killed them so quickly?"

"Are you sure you're not aware of anything that could take out a horde of vampires?" Desportan wondered.

"No. I've never encountered something like this before. This. This is all new to me."

Everyone lowered their weapons and sat down. The silence was deafening to them. Brant entered the kitchen and grabbed a beer. Taking a drink to calm himself.

"What now?" Aldon wondered.

"He knows we're here." Abelard said. "We must move quickly to avoid his grasp."

"Move? And go where?"

"Anywhere but here. This place is compromised."

From the door came the same rushing wind as before. Grabbing their attention to the fullest as Brant and Donn made their way toward the door with the shotgun and arrow prepped. Behind them stood Eddie, Aldon, and Desportan while Abelard, Lucy, and Anna kept their sights on the windows. Their weapons aimed. The silent air kept them focused, yet a slight shiver of the bones brought a speck of fear within the home.

"Come on you bastards." Brant whispered.

The door had opened to their surprise to see nothing. Before they could check the door, a figure's foot entered with one quiet step. Abelard stood up as he saw the figure enter the home. Cloaked in black from neck to feet. Hands twitching with its nails. Eyes sparked like lightning. Yet there was an intelligence behind the eyes. The others were ready to bring fire upon the visitor.

"What are you?" Abelard questioned as the figure stood at the door.

"Hey, Doc." Brant said. "How come this thing looks like one of them?"

"But it's not." Abelard said. "Aren't you?"

"No." The figure said with a whisper. "I am not like the others."

"How can we believe that?" Aldon said. "Look at it. Pale skin. Sharp fangs and nails. It's a vampire."

"The eyes." Abelard noted. "They're not red."

"They're gold." Desportan said.

Donn looked at the group before turning his eyes toward the visitor. The bow was pulled and the arrow was set. The visitor moved its eyes to see their weaponry and chuckled at the sight of the bow.

"You can lower your weapon. Such will not harm me."

"I'll take my chances."

Abelard stepped forward to get a closer look at the visitor. The visitor was indeed a vampire. Yet, a vampire to which was only a mystery to Abelard. He's never encountered one with golden eyes.

"What kind are you?"

"I am something more. Something the others fear just as the humans."

"It was you." Lucy said. "You killed those vampires outside."

"My army did. I was only a witness to the battle."

"Your army?" Desportan said.

"Yes. They're here. Surrendering this home. But do not worry. I've signaled them to only attack the vampires of the opposite ends. Humans are not a primary target of my kind."

"You don't kill humans?" Brant asked. "Seriously?"

"I do not. I and my army only feast on animals. Humans are not our concern. The others are."

"The other vampires." Abelard said. "Then, you're familiar with the Dark One."

The visitor breathed in by the notion of that name and exhaled to satisfaction.

"I know where he is."

"You do?" Abelard jumped. "Where is he? Where's the Dark One located?"

The eyes of Abelard widen. His curiosity was peaked as he wanted to know the location.

"I will tell you where he is. It seems we're all on the same side of this fight."

"You're on the side of humanity?" Desportan said.

"I am on the side in which takes out the Dark One and his forces."

"So there's some kind of vampire turf war going on that we didn't know about." Brant said. "That's great. Good to know."

"Once the Dark One is defeated, the war is not over."

"What are you talking about?" Abelard questioned. "The Dark One is the one who started all of this. He's the key to ending this."

"He started this, yes. But, he is not the end. The others are."

"What. Others."

"The Fated Ones. The Dark One is only one in that order. What he's seeking to do is awaken the others. If they rise up, all of your world is nearing the end at a quicker rate. Myself and my army were designed to challenge the Fated Ones as an opposition to keep the balance. Now, it is the time."

Abelard slammed his weapon in anger. Desportan went to calm him, but Abelard would not hearken to him or his words.

"We do not have much time. We must end this tonight. Before the sun rises."

"Tell us where he is."

"He's at the State Capital. Dwelling within with his army of Hordes."

"Why's he inside the Capital building?"

"He's about to quake the earth. He's chosen this place as the beginning of the end."

Abelard walked away, heading upstairs. Desportan questioned him, but was given no response. The visitor noticed Abelard's seriousness of the battle and respected the elder. He glanced at Desportan who was checking on Lucy.

"Keep each other close. For a time is coming where it will be a challenge."

"He's a fortune teller now." Brant joked.

"I've been told over the centuries. My words deem true in the end."

Abelard returned downstairs with his gear.

"What are you doing?" Desportan asked.

"I'm going to the Capital building. We have to end this. He's right."

"You're going to trust this thing?"

"He's a vampire I've never encountered. I sense honor within him. He desires the same thing I do: to end the Dark One and this plague he's created."

Brant nodded as he looked over to Donn. The two stood up and went beside Abelard. Desportan knew they were going as well. Anna also walked over and stood beside Abelard. Desportan sighed.

"If we do this, we're only going to stop the Dark One and end this."

"I agree." The visitor said.

"Your name." Abelard said. "All vampires seem to have a name. what's yours?"

"I go by the name, Aldrik."

Abelard nodded.

"Aldrik. I am Professor Abelard Ekkehardt."

"I know who you are. I've seen your work over in the East. It's what drew me here. To aid someone like you in this fight. We share a common enemy. Or enemies."

"Everyone." Desportan said. "Grab your gear. We're heading out."

Everyone followed Desportan's order as Abelard walked

outside, following Aldrik. Desportan was concerned, yet Brant had it covered as he and Donn followed them both. Everyone was prepared as they stepped outside the home, seeing Aldrik speaking with Abelard. The sight of a vampire on their side was eerie. But there was trust between Ekkehardt and Aldrik. Desportan could see it clearly.

Brant and Donn glanced around the trees and saw more golden eyes glinting in the shadows. They knew it was Aldrik's army. There was no gnawing of teeth or screeches. Just the eyes.

Now, what's the plan?" Desportan questioned.

"I will meet you all at the Capital building. There we can strategize our plan."

"I agree." Abelard said.

Aldrik nodded to the group before leaping into the air, vanishing from their sight into the night sky. Behind him was his army, all rising up from the trees and disappearing into the darkness.

"Very well." Abelard said. "Let's end this."

CHAPTER EIGHT

The group arrived at the State Capital, seeing the place surrounded by Dunkan's vampires. Dozens on the field while several scattered across the rooftop.

"What's the plan?" Brant asked.

"Where's Aldrik?" Desportan said.

"He'll be here." Abelard replied. "I can sense he's a man of his word."

Brant loaded the shotgun. Prepared to approach the Capital building. Before taking one step further, the wind bellowed above them. Grabbing their attention as they saw Aldrik and his vampire army. Making his landing in front of them as the vampires hover in the air, their eyes glinting toward Dunkan's own.

"Seems you've all arrived." Aldrik said.

"How do we get inside." Abelard asked. "I want to face the Dark One now."

"He's got it heavily guarded inside. It won't be easy to confront him without taking down his army."

"Inside, where is the Dark One?" Desportan questioned.

"Standing. Under the dome."

Brant watched as Dunkan's vampires began to notice their movement from across the pathways.

"How do we dealt with the vamps surrounding the building? We can't just all go blazing toward them. They'll take us out within minutes."

"Leave the vampires to my army. Here is the plan: my Dreaded Ones will take the battle to the Dark One's vampires while all of you make your way inside. There, eliminate any vampires which may target you as some of mine will also be inside to assist you."

"How can we tell?" Eddie said.

"The eyes mark the sides." Aldrik said with his golden eyes glinting.

"What about the Dark One?" Abelard said. "When we confront him-"

"When we do, I will be there to face him alongside you. It will take several of us to defeat him. Something myself cannot do alone."

"Best we move quick. Daylight is only a matter of minutes away."

"Then, I suggest we begin." Aldrik grinned. "Go forth, my army! Feast on the corpses of the adversary!"

The Dreaded Ones moved with speed as they began the assault on Dunkan's vampires. Through the loud tears of flesh and screeches of horror, the team led by Desportan ran for the entrance into the Capital. Through their rushing speed, several of Dunkan's vampires noticed them and went to strike only to be decapitated by Anna and Abelard. Reaching the front door, Desportan went to open it, only to find it locked.

"Can't get in."

"What do you mean you can't get in?" Brant said.

"The door's locked. Or jammed. He doesn't want us inside."

Abelard grunted, turning around toward their surrounding, seeing the vampire-on-vampire warfare. From the sky fell three vampires to Aldrik's landing, wiping their blood from his mouth. He saw them at the door.

"Some help would be useful." Abelard nodded.

Aldrik yelled for them to move away from the door as he spearheaded it with his shoulder, blasting it from the hinges. The group entered with Desportan and Abelard thanking the leader of the Dreaded Ones. Standing inside, the group found themselves surrounded by more of Dunkan's vampires as Abelard moved through them with his blade. Anna followed him to the other's surprise. Brant and Donn used their shotgun and arrows to fend off the coming vampires.

"Where is the Dark One?!" Abelard screamed.

"There." Aldrik pointed. "That way."

Abelard went toward the direction, only to be stopped by Desportan.

"What are you doing?"

"Yu can't go rushing into this fight. Not by yourself."

"Then, step aside and follow me!"

"I agree with the Professor on this one." Brant responded after shooting one of the vampires.

Desportan sighed and nodded. Abelard agreed as they followed him down the path. While the others handled the vampires along with Aldrik's army, Desportan, Abelard, Brant, and Aldrik proceeded to face the Dark One as they entered the domain of his residence. Within the room, Abelard saw him standing under the dome of the interior. The Dark One's eyes lit up like a burning flame toward them. The sight of Aldrik seared within his eyes as he stepped forward.

"We meet again."

"This time it will be the last." Abelard yelled.

"Something you've continued to say ever since we've shared encounters. Oh, Professor, how will your life come to an end if it isn't by my hands."

"He's not alone." Aldrik said. "I've been looking or you as well."

"You! You align yourself with his Creation? Of all things a

vampire never desires to do."

"You are this world's enemy. You and your brothers. With my aid, I will help humanity send you all into the depths of the Flame."

"Now is your chance to see it through. Face me and let's end this."

The group lunged toward Dunkan with all they had. But, it was not enough. Brant's shotgun was quickly snapped in two by Dunkan's strength, Desportan's gun was crushed and Abelard's blade was broken. Leaving Aldrik and his strength to combat the Dark One. The two vampires stared blows of punches and swipes of claws. Both bleeding from their quickened wounds. Their movement was in such a speed, the others could not comprehend what was taking place. The two vampires only appeared like bolting shadows sparking in the colors of red and gold in their sight. Abelard looked at the hilt of his broken blade and went to strike Dunkan. Running into the battle, Dunkan caught him and twisted the elder man's arm before tossing him to the floor. Desportan ran o aid him as Dunkan caught Aldrik by he throat, lifting him up into the air and slamming him into the floor. Cracking it deeply.

"You're no match for one such as I." Dunkan said toward Aldrik.

"I have something you do not possess. Integrity."

Dunkan reached into his cloak and raised up a staff made of glistened stone. The staff's head was made of gold and had the appearance of an angel. An angel with demonic wings and sharp fangs similar to his own. Abelard saw it and pointed with his left arm in horror.

"He has it. *The Staff of the Grigori.*"

Dunkan held the staff above the beaten and bloody body of Aldrik.

"This new day as the sun rises, I will summon forth my

brethren and together, shall we shroud this world in darkness and conquer it as our own."

"You can rise up your brothers." Aldrik said. "But, you will never rule this world."

Dunkan held the staff and began speaking in a language none of them could understand. Once he was finished, he glared down toward Aldrik in disgust.

"With your blood, my brothers shall rise again!"

The staff lowered and slammed the staff into the heart of Aldrik. Killing him and his Dreaded Ones as immediately after, an earthquake began. The earthquake was powerful to the point the Capital began to crack and fall. Desportan helped Abelard escape as the others were already outside. Dunkan stood under the dome and laughed at the scenery.

"Now it is time. Now, my brothers shall rise once again.

The group were all outside as they watched the Capital collapse. However, little did they know, across the world, Dunkan's brethren had awoken. In such lands like Egypt, Iran, Turkey, Chile, India, and Mongolia. The sky around them became consumed with darkness as the sun rose, yet was hidden by an eclipse. Abelard witnessed it and sighed bitterly.

"What's happening?" Brant wondered. "What's going on?"

"It's happened." Abelard said.

"What's happened?" Desportan questioned.

"*The Ancients Have Risen.*"

CREED: HELL RISEN

I

BURNING SENSATION

One night across the city of Hartford, Connecticut in the span of only a few hours, calls were rung into the authorities over a mass murder. The murders had seemed to be committed all at one time across the entire city. Even into the suburb areas. With the police unable to track down a concrete source to continue their investigation, hovering over the city throughout the bleak clouds was Creed, The Unholy Knight. Gleaming down toward the city, Creed moved with speed and a supernatural form of stealth. His appearance unseen by the eyes of the living due to the illusion conjured by his flowing midnight-blue cape.

"These bodies." Creed examined. "They're charred. Poor souls."

The victims were all burnt. Their skin bubbling continually as the sound of cracks sparked. Even in the presence of the officers and coroners. The heat coming from their bodies was too hot for the coroners to continue their work further. Choosing to leave the bodies in their discovered state, Creed searched them all. Seeing everybody was burnt in similar fashion. Knowing it all took place at one time, Creed knew there wasn't a natural solution to the cause. Hearing the willowing sound from behind him, Creed rose up from his knee, seeing Ananchel standing beside him looking down over the bodies. Beaming of light.

"You've found them." She said.

"I have. These weren't natural deaths. Something reeks of this cause."

"I know who's responsible. But, you're not familiar with the murderer."

"Speak the name."

"You smell the stench in the air?"

"I do. Smells of brimstone. Only hellfire could've done such a thing."

"Sinfire also has its bidding." Ananchel mentioned. "However, you are correct. Hellfire is the cause of their deaths. The officers won't be able to answer the families of the victims with sound information."

"They will do what they can." Creed said. "Meanwhile, you said you know who's responsible. Tell me who."

"A demon. Calls itself *Brimstone*."

"Leaving its mark for us to find. Not a smart demon."

"Don't think of him lightly. Brimstone has been around through the ages. He's responsible for great fires in the ancient past. Myself and the Cherubim did our best to cool his wrath. Fortunately, we did and he was driven into hiding."

"And now he's risen again to cause more hell." Creed spoke. "By what means has caused him to be risen?"

"I do not know. Perhaps, he's risen due to the growing power of the Cryptic Zone."

"You believe Adrambadon has a hand in this?"

"I'm not saying such. Only implying the Zone is surging with power. All of the air across the earth is mucked in mysticism. Most of us are not sure why nor do we know the source's location."

Creed took another look at the bodies and he watched as the officers continued their work to the best of their ability. The coroners even went to the point of dousing water over the bodies to cool them. Yet, the water only increased their burnt nature with sparks emitting from the cracked skin.

"What must be done?" Creed asked.

"Brimstone moves with speed. Speed beyond most of ours. Yet, you may be able to catch up to him."

"Do you have a precise location of his whereabouts?"

"I do not. I know he likes a challenge. Given by any means, he'll accept a challenge if it deems itself powerful enough to test him."

"His figure? What does this Brimstone appear to be?"

"Unlike Satanic, he's not a dog-like being. More so one of them."

"He's in the image like the sons of Adam?"

"Yes. Appearing like one of them is what gives him an edge."

"And I'm assuming he's burning in nature?"

"Like a flowing volcano after an explosion."

Creed took a nod and flew into the air, searching Hartford. Through his eyes, he spotted an open field. The moment was set in motion.

"I'll call him out. See what he's made of."

"And where will you do this?" Ananchel wondered.

"There's an open field over in the distance. Far from humans. There, I shall call out this Brimstone and end his little run."

"Calling him out is a challenge he'll accept."

"You know of this?" Creed wondered. "You're saying such an act is simple for him?"

"He loves challenges. Once you call him out, he'll appear. He can't resist."

II

THE WARNING OF THE UNDERWORLD

Creed flown into the open field. Nothing but trees surrounding him. Stretching out his arms, Creed began to recite a ritual in the language of the Cryptic Zone. The ground trembled as it cracked open, unveiling the glooming glow of the Cryptic Zone. Through such power, Creed was able to expand his power, absorbing the energy flowing from the Cryptic Zone into his being. Closing his hands together, the cracks sealed, and the trembles ceased.

"Brimstone! I summon you to this place! Leave humanity be and face me!"

Through the quietness of the wind circling the field, the ground quaked once more, however not through Creed's own power. Certain of this, Creed's gaze turned every corner as through the ground erupted a geyser of flames. Standing back as his cape shielded him from the fires, within them stepped out Brimstone himself. Creed paused as his cape moved from his eyes, Brimstone's appearance was just as Ananchel told him.

"This is the famed Unholy Knight." Brimstone growled.

"I am he you have spoke. See you've come to my calling."

"Indeed I have. I can only believe Ananchel gave you such an idea to begin with. Although, it is a pity she couldn't do the work herself. Nor any of the angels above."

"Your business is with me. Not with the angels."

"I am aware. Yet, you have to be wondering why I've come at such a strange time."

"You killed those innocents. Burned their bodies to cinders."

"Only to gain someone's attention. Didn't matter whose it was, only that my work received its reward."

"A reward of what nature?" Creed questioned. "A treasure?"

"I have no need of treasures. I sought out another in the spiritual warfare and you answered the call."

"You sought out a battle. To test your own skills against another."

"Yes. And what better skills to be tested than the Cryptic powers against the fires of Hell itself!"

Creed's claws formed over his fingers as his cape whipped across the air. A bellowing, powerful gust against Brimstone as the fires covering his body wisped away, slowly reappearing in mass as the embers emerged. Brimstone waved his hand while shaking his head. A grin of sinister faces grew on his face. Creed's eyes remained focus.

"You haven't truly questioned the reason for all of this." Brimstone said. "Your battle against Medieval proved to all of us that you have such skills yet to be fully revealed."

"How do you know about Medieval?"

"Because we know everyone and their reasons in such fields. Medieval deals with warfare while I tend to the flames. It's only nature in action."

"I've heard enough. I'm ending your actions above this ground."

"Do your best. However, why don't we take it below."

"Below?" Creed said.

Brimstone raised his arms, causing the ground to tremble. The trembles increased as Creed leaped up into the air to maintain his balance. Gazing down, he saw the ground had opened and through his eyes, he was looking into Hell itself. Brimstone chuckled at the sight, whipping fire into his hands.

"Let us see if the cryptic power can match the fires of Hell!"

Moving like lightning, Brimstone struck Creed in the face with the fire blast and dragged the Unholy Knight down into the pit. Once they were several feet deep, the ground above them had sealed. Now, Creed crashed onto the ground, surrounded by flames. The flames were the color of his cape and sparked like the gold of his eyes. Creed stood up and took a moment to see his surroundings as Brimstone was nowhere to be found.

"Ah." Creed said. "So, this is Hell."

III

HELLFIRE

Creed hovered over the fires of Hell, hearing the fainted cries of the souls within the burning flames. Gazing down over them, he could recognize their human nature as they shouted to him to warn their families. Creed hung his head hearing their cries for the living. However, Creed knew his words wouldn't matter to the living and he continued searching for Brimstone.

"Where is he?" Creed questioned within.

A gusher of flames emitted from the fire in front of Creed, hitting him from below as he tumbled through the air, regaining his balance. Taking a look around the flames and the molten rock surrounding him, Brimstone rushed toward him like a lightning bolt of fire, striking him in the chest with a deepening punch. Creed fell and crashed onto the ground, surrounded by the sapphire-glowing flames as Brimstone stepped down in front of him.

"Welcome to my domain!" Brimstone cocked.

"It appears you are afraid of what's above. Proclaiming this prison as your domain."

"Me and the fires are one. Otherwise, I would not exist."

"And you sought to attack those of the earth only for the pursuit of a challenge."

"A challenge which you accepted. Now, shall we continue this bout before you give in to your own concerns."

"I will defeat you, demon and afterwards, I will cleanse the disturbance you have brought upon those families."

"Heh. Good luck with that."

Brimstone and Creed clashed with blows to the jaws and chest. Jumping back a few feet, Brimstone rushed against Creed with his heel, striking Creed in the face and latching his hands to Creed's ankles, tripping him onto reground as he face came close to the burning fires. With a quick grunt, Creed kicked himself up and conjured a sword from his hands, impressing Brimstone.

"You think you're the only one who can wield such power?!"

Brimstone repeated Creed's own actions, forming a molten sword from his hands. Creed held his steady as Brimstone leaped into the air, crashing down against Creed's sword. The two struggled against one another with their strength. Creed's golden eyes flickered as Brimstone's face morphed between human and demon forms. Droplets of fire fell from Brimstone's head onto Creed's face, burning him for a few seconds. Creed shoved Brimstone from him, twirling the blade as he cut Brimstone's chest with the tip of the sword. A chuckle came out of Brimstone's mouth before he slashed Creed's abdomen with his own sword, burning him in the process.

"I'm not even tired, Cryptic One!"

"Neither am I."

Creed's cape bellowed around him before spanning out like wings of a great dragon, picking up the fires from around them and tossing them against Brimstone. The fiery demon used his sword to swipe down the incoming fireballs as Creed took the chance and speared Brimstone against the molten walls with his sword.

"Argh!" Brimstone grunted. "You think this will defeat me?!"

"No." Creed answered. "But it gives me the chance to keep you down here. At least for a while."

Creed raised his right hand, from his sharp fingertips emerged a golden hue of energy. Taking the focus of the energy, Creed directed it from his hand toward Brimstone. The golden energy warped into a liquid form, seemly unharmed by the flames of Hell. Brimstone pulled the sword from his shoulder as the energy surrounded him. Wrapping itself around him against eh wall like a snake to its prey. Feeling the tightness of the energy, Brimstone yelled with a deepen scream. Not one of pain, but of anger.

"What is this?!" Brimstone screamed. "What have you done?!"

"I've used a portion of my Cryptic powers to trap you here. In Hell."

"You cannot trap me! I was formed from this realm!"

"I know and the power of the Cryptic Zone will make sure you remain here until the end of days."

"No. No! I will not be trapped by some disgruntled figure! A human made into a Crypticoid!"

Creed turned away, looking up toward what appeared to be a sparking light. Creed focused on the light through Brimstone's continued yelling and flew into the air toward the light. Inching closer, Creed discovered the light was a pathway for him to return to the earth and he went through the light, quickly finding himself above the ground and in the skies overlooking the field where he fell into the pit. Seeing the field, Creed noticed there was no hole where he fell.

"I'm back."

Hearing wings behind him, Creed quickly turned to see Ananchel moving with a haste in her flight. Her face slightly bruised with her wings bleeding from beneath and claw makes against her chest armor. Her eyes only told of a horror Creed had never seen. Ananchel attempted to keep her balance in the air, yet she fell to the ground. Creed flew down and caught her before she crashed.

"What happened?" Creed asked. "What's going on?"

"Something's wrong... the powers... they've been... altered."

"Powers? What powers?"

"The mystical energy that surrounds the universe. Something has altered them and now, they've been awoken."

"Who's been awoken?"

"The Dark Gods. I tried to help the sorcerer, but their powers were too great."

"Sorcerer?"

"Go now, Creed and help him."

"Help who?"

"*The Supreme Enchanter. Doctor Fortune.*"

THE STORY OF ABELARD EKKEHARDT, ALLAN
DESPORTAN, LUCY SEWARD, ANNA IIARIO, BRANT
WADE, AND THE DARK ONE WILL CONCLUDE IN:

OUR SEALED FATE

THE THIRD AND FINAL INSTALLMENT OF *THE HORDE*
TRILOGY

ABOUT THE AUTHOR

Ty'Ron W. C. Robinson II is the author of several works of fiction. Including the *Dark Titan Universe Saga*, *The Haunted City Saga*, *EverWar Universe*, *Symbolum Venatores*, *Frightened!*, *Instincts*, and others. More information pertaining to the author and stories can be found at darktitanentertainment.com.

Twitter: @DarkTitan_
Instagram: @darktitanentertainment
Facebook: @DarkTitanEnt
Pinterest: @darktitanentertainment
YouTube: Dark Titan Entertainment

www.ingramcontent.com/pod-product-compliance
Lightning Source LLC
LaVergne TN
LVHW041558070526
838199LV00046B/2031